FRANKIE'S MAGIC FOOTBALL

FRANKIE AND THE DRAGON CURSE

FRANK LAMPARD

LITTLE, BROWN BOOKS FOR YOUNG READERS
www.lbkids.co.uk

LITTLE, BROWN BOOKS FOR YOUNG READERS

First published in Great Britain in 2014 by Little, Brown Books
for Young Readers

Copyright © 2014 by Lamps On Productions

The moral right of the author has been asserted.

A CIP catalogue record for this book
is available from the British Library.

ISBN 978-0-349-12446-9

Typeset in Cantarell by M Rules
Printed and bound in Great Britain by
Clays Ltd, St Ives plc

Papers used by LBYR are from well-managed forests
and other responsible sources.

MIX
Paper from
responsible sources
FSC® C104740

Little, Brown Books for Young Readers
An imprint of
Little, Brown Book Group
100 Victoria Embankment
London EC4Y 0DY

An Hachette UK Company
www.hachette.co.uk

www.lbkids.co.uk

To my mum Pat, who encouraged me to do my homework in between kicking a ball all around the house, and is still with me every step of the way.

*Welcome to a fantastic
Fantasy League — the greatest
football competition ever held
in this world or any other!*

*You'll need four on a team,
so choose carefully. This is a lot
more serious than a game in the
park. You'll never know who your
next opponents will be, or
where you'll face them.*

*So lace up your boots, players,
and good luck! The whistle's
about to blow!*

The Ref

CHAPTER 1

It was raining hard as Frankie, Louise and Charlie ran along the pavement. Max, Frankie's dog, was on his lead and scampered to keep up.

"Nearly there now!" called Louise.

She turned into a doorway next to a Chinese supermarket, and

Frankie and Charlie piled in after her.

"Welcome to the Chinese Cultural Centre," said Louise.

They were standing in a foyer, and there were posters on a noticeboard advertising everything from lessons in Mandarin to restaurants to travel agents. Louise's gran was Chinese, and Louise came here a lot. Max shook himself dry and looked up at Frankie with a bedraggled face.

"We're early," said Louise, looking around. "Maybe my sifu isn't here yet."

"What's a *sifu*?" asked Charlie.

"It's the name we give to the kung fu teacher," Louise replied. She took off her coat and hung it on a peg. As Frankie did the same, she pointed to Max. "He'd better stay out here. I'm not sure he can take part in the kung fu class."

Max cocked his head as if he was insulted and Frankie laughed. He was looking forward to trying something new. Louise had been learning the martial art for two years, so she'd already completed lots of grades. Underneath her coat she was wearing a black kung fu suit with white cuffs and toggles across the front.

Frankie's eyes widened as he spotted Charlie peeling off his goalie gloves. Louise gasped too.

"What are you doing?" she asked.

Charlie shrugged. "I didn't think I could wear them in the class."

"You can't," she said. "But you *never* take them off!"

"Yeah," said Frankie. "You say goalkeepers always need to be ready."

Charlie sighed. "I'm not a goalkeeper any more though, am I?"

Frankie shared a look with

Louise. He knew why his friend was in such a sad mood. Charlie had let in four goals against the Basset Road team earlier in the week. One had been really embarrassing, because he'd tripped over his own feet.

"We all have bad games," said Louise, putting her arm around Charlie's shoulder. "Perhaps the kung fu will help with your balance and positioning. It's not all chops and kicks, you know."

Charlie gave a small smile. "It can't make me any worse."

Frankie had never seen him so glum.

"Come on, I'll show you the training room," said Louise.

She slid open a door and they walked into a large room with mats on the floor and a mirror covering the whole wall at one end. On the other walls, there were pictures of men and women doing high kicks and strange moves, and lots of painted Chinese lettering that Frankie didn't understand.

But the most impressive thing in the room was a huge decorated dragon. It seemed to be made of cardboard and paper, with frills and horns and multi-coloured scales. It had golden eyes that scowled under its arched brows.

"Wow!" he said.

"We use it at festivals," said Louise. "It takes four or five people to lift it, and they perform a dragon dance."

"It looks scary!" said Charlie.

"Not at all," said a voice behind them. A small man in a suit similar to Louise's stepped into the room, folding an umbrella. He had a newspaper tucked under his arm.

"Sifu Tan!" said Louise. She gave a bow, with her hands clasped together.

The old man put down the

paper and the umbrella on a table and bowed in return. "Hello, Louise. These must be your friends Charlie and Frankie." Sifu Tan frowned. "But which one is which? I heard that Charlie always wore gloves, even in bed at night."

Charlie blushed and didn't say anything, so Frankie stepped in. "He's Charlie," he said, pointing at his friend. "I'm Frankie."

Max barked. "And that's Max," said Frankie.

Sifu Tan bowed to them then picked up the newspaper again. "I hear you're both as keen on football as Louise. This might interest you."

As he unfolded the paper, Frankie saw that the writing was all in Chinese script. The front cover picture showed a boy not much older than him, standing beside a football which was resting on a cushion.

"What's it about?" said Frankie. "Is that boy some sort of star football player in China?"

Louise looked over the sifu's shoulder. "The headline says 'Proof! China invented football!'"

"I always thought we invented football in England," said Frankie.

Louise read on. "Apparently, the boy discovered an ancient porcelain football buried in his garden. Scientists think it's over two thousand years old!"

"What's the point of a football made out of pottery?" said Charlie. "It would break!"

"They think it might have been

just for decoration," said Louise, laughing. "There are twelve panels, all showing different creatures in the Chinese Zodiac. It's been bought by a museum and they're going to put it on show."

Frankie stared at the picture. "I'd love to see it!" he gasped.

"Bet it's not as good as your football," said Charlie with a wink, nodding towards Frankie's rucksack. Frankie kept the magic football with him now, in case his brother Kevin tried to get his hands on it to cause mischief.

The sifu stretched his arms. "Looks like no one else is coming," he said. "We should warm up before practice. How about we use your football for some exercises, Frankie?"

Frankie felt a rush of panic. What if the football decided to do something magical? "Er . . . I'm not sure . . ."

"Come on," said the sifu. "Until today, I would have said it wasn't traditional to use a ball in kung fu. But now I've read that newspaper article, it might be fun. I was quite a good player in my youth."

Frankie reluctantly took out the ball and handed it to Sifu Tan.

"Right!" said the teacher. "Let's

start by running in a circle around the room."

Max waited by the door while they set off. Sifu Tan stood in the centre of the hall, kicking the ball out for them to pass back. Then they'd swap positions, or change direction. Soon Frankie was working up a sweat.

Somewhere, a phone rang. "Excuse me" said Sifu Tan. "Why don't you throw it to each other, to warm up your arms." He left the room.

"He's very fit for an old man," said Charlie, bending over and breathing hard.

"He's been practising kung fu since he was three years old," said Louise. "Here, catch this!"

She threw the ball to Charlie, but he jumped too short. It arced straight for the paper dragon.

Oh no! thought Frankie. He saw his own horrified expression in the mirror.

The ball dropped right into the dragon's mouth.

At the same moment, the mirror's surface began to buckle and his reflection blurred. It looked as though the glass was melting.

"Something's happening!" said Louise.

Frankie's skin tingled. "It's the football's magic," he said. As the room around them became distorted, he was sure the dragon winked at him. Then everything vanished in a flash of light.

CHAPTER 2

Frankie felt a light breeze on his face. He blinked, and as his vision cleared, he saw that he was standing before a huge arched gateway. It was painted red, orange and green. Louise and Charlie were at his side, and Max stood at his feet, panting.

"It's happened again, hasn't it?" said Charlie. "Where are we this time?"

"The Forbidden City!" said Louise, looking around. "I recognise it from my dad's photo album. We're in China."

"I love Chinese food," yapped Max.

Frankie jumped. It always surprised him when Max started speaking, but it was just part of the football's magic.

"Chinese food doesn't love you," said Frankie. "Remember that time you ate all the leftovers from the takeaway off the kitchen table? We had to take you to the vet!"

"It was worth it," said Max. "Crispy duck – yum!"

They wandered through the gateway, gazing up at the beautiful buildings. Wide open courtyards and broad steps led up to pagodas painted in gold and red. There were shrines surrounded by columns, and green ponds so still that Frankie could see his reflection in the water. For once, he realised, the ball's magic hadn't changed his clothes. He was still wearing the same red sweatshirt and shorts from back home.

"I wonder why the magic football

brought us to the Forbidden City?" said Louise.

"Where *is* the football?" said Charlie.

Frankie shrugged. Normally they had it with them, but he couldn't see it anywhere. "Who knows? Maybe we don't need . . ." He tailed off as his eyes landed on a poster tacked to the side of a bridge. It showed the porcelain football in full colour. "Perhaps that's why we're here," he said.

Louise read the poster. "It's in the palace museum!"

"Let's go and have a look," said Frankie.

It wasn't hard to find the museum, a three-storey building at the top of a huge set of steps. There were plenty of tourists standing in long queues. Just as they reached the top of the steps, Frankie heard an explosion of broken glass from above. Everyone looked up, shouting. Green smoke poured from several second-storey windows. Almost at once, a shrill alarm sounded.

"Uh-oh," said Charlie. "Something tells me that isn't good."

Security guards surrounded the front of a building, blowing whistles and waving their arms.

They began to marshal panicked
visitors out of the museum. People
were snapping pictures on their
phones.

"We should go inside," said
Frankie.

"Maybe we should mind our own
business," said Charlie.

"Frankie's right," said Louise.

"The football brought us here for a reason. But how can we get past the guards?"

"Leave it to me," said Max. He charged off between people's feet. With his jaws, he grabbed one of the tapes that kept visitors in line. Frankie lost sight of him among the forest of legs, but the security guards were peering at the ground, shouting to one another. They certainly weren't paying attention to Frankie and his friends. Max's plan had worked.

"Let's go!" Frankie said.

They darted through the open

doors of the museum into an empty hall. The alarms were even louder here, making Frankie's ears ring. Louise snatched up a flyer and quickly read it. "The football is on display upstairs!" she said.

Max arrived by their side, skidding across the marble floor. "Good job, boy," said Frankie.

They ran to the stairs opposite, when the doors of an elevator pinged and started to open. Frankie pointed to some cushioned seats in the middle of the hall and they all crouched behind them. Frankie peered around the edge of a seat.

A young woman in a suit stepped out of the escalator, with another security guard. She was speaking fast.

"Keep all the doors locked," she said. "No one comes in or out until we know what triggered the alarm."

She strode towards an office marked "private" and disappeared inside. Frankie straightened up and headed for the stairs again.

On the first floor, the museum was deserted. Suddenly the alarms died, leaving only the sound of their hurried footsteps. They ran past several galleries where there were

ornate vases, embroidered wall-
hangings, and ancient weapons
and armour. Louise led them to a
room at the end of a corridor, then
checked the plan again on the flyer.
"I think it should be in here," she
said.

Frankie went first, edging
through the door. The room was
filled with the same drifting green
smoke he'd seen from the steps
outside. Max brushed past his
ankles.

"Wait!" Frankie whispered. "We
don't know what's in there."

A huge shape passed through the
smoke like a shadow. Frankie saw

it pause by a glass case containing
a round object on a plinth. *The
porcelain football!*

SMASH! The figure had swung
a gloved fist at the glass case. It
leant in to grab the artefact. Frankie
shouted, "Hey, stop!"

As the smoke cleared, the figure
turned round. Frankie felt a cold
wave sweep through him. The
man wore head-to-toe armour,
hundreds of overlapping panels of
rusted bronze. On his head was a
helmet made of the same metal.
All Frankie could see through the
visor was a pair of dark, hate-filled
eyes.

"What are you doing?" asked
Frankie.

The warrior grabbed the football
under one arm. "Zha-Hu cannot be
stopped!" he growled, then strode
towards a broken window. Frankie
dashed after him, feet crunching
over the broken glass.

"There's nowhere to run!"
Frankie called.

The man reached the window
and leapt up on to the sill. Frankie's
blood ran cold. "Don't jump!" he
said. "It's too far down!"

The figure stared at him blankly,
then fell backwards.

Frankie leapt to try to grab him,

but it was too late. He stuck his head through the broken window, just as Louise and Charlie arrived at his side.

Frankie couldn't believe what he was seeing.

The man hadn't fallen far at all. He had landed on something that hovered just beneath the window ledge. It was a creature with a broad scaly back, and two black wings that stretched wide. A creature with a head tapering in a black snout, and a long tail that waved back and forth.

A creature that Frankie *knew* didn't exist outside of story books.

"What are you all looking at?" said Max, paws on Frankie's leg. "Did he get squished?"

Frankie swallowed. "No, boy. He's sitting on a dragon!"

CHAPTER 3

"Ha ha," said Max. "I might be a dog, but I'm not stupid."

Frankie picked Max up and rested him on the window sill, just in time to see the dragon turn and swoop low over the buildings of the Forbidden City.

Max whimpered.

Soon the dragon that carried the soldier was just a distant dot soaring up towards the cloudy sky.

"Wow – that dragon looks just like the ones on the vases in the museum," said Charlie.

Max's ears pricked. "Someone's coming," he said.

Frankie glanced over his shoulder and saw several people approaching from the corridor. There were three security guards and the woman from earlier.

"Stop right there!" she said. "You're in a lot of trouble."

Frankie glanced around at

the smoke-filled room and the shattered glass case. He wasn't sure how they'd explain this one.

Ten minutes later, they were all sitting in the empty café area on the museum's top floor. The tables were still littered with abandoned plates of food and drinks. The woman in the suit was standing in the doorway, looking annoyed. A gruff, middle-aged man, the head of security, sat opposite them.

"So, you expect me to believe this?" he said. "An armoured man flew away with the museum's property on the back of a dragon?"

Frankie and his friends nodded. Thankfully, Max stayed quiet. A talking dog would not help the situation.

Each time Frankie told the story, it seemed more ridiculous.

The head of security shook his head. "I see no choice but to call your parents. They'll be

worried about you. Are they in the Forbidden City too?"

"Erm . . . not exactly," said Frankie.

"A hotel, then?" said the man.

"They aren't with us," said Louise. "This is a . . . school trip."

The man folded his arms. "Right, who's your teacher?"

Louise fell silent, but Charlie blurted out, "Sifu Tan."

The security man scribbled the name in a notepad from his top pocket. He looked up. "And does this Mr Tan have a phone number?"

"Please," said Frankie. "You don't need to call anyone. Just let us go."

"Not until you tell us the truth," said the head of security. "Who was your accomplice? He must have the ball. How did he escape?"

"We told you," said Charlie. "On a dragon!"

The security guard's shoulders sagged. "Unless you can give me something else, I'll have to summon the police to deal with you."

Frankie remembered another detail. "The man said something about 'Zha-Hu'. He said 'Zha-Hu cannot be stopped'."

As soon as the name left his mouth, the woman by the door stepped forwards.

"Perhaps I could speak to these children alone?" she said.

"Can't do any harm," said the security guard. "Just let me know when to bring in the police."

He shuffled out of the room, leaving them alone. The woman locked the door. *Strange*, thought Frankie.

"My name is Lin," she said, turning back to them. "I'm the curator of the museum."

"Hello," said Frankie. "I'm sorry about your football going missing, but you have to believe us."

"As a matter of fact," said the curator, "I'm beginning to."

"*Really?*" said Charlie.

Lin nodded. "I was desperate for the museum to buy the football at first," she said. "But as soon as it was here, I felt very odd about it — scared even."

"Scared of a football?" said Louise.

The woman smiled. "And now you mention Zha-Hu, it makes perfect sense."

"Does it?" said Charlie.

The curator glanced towards the door. "We don't have long before my head of security becomes suspicious. Zha-Hu was an evil warrior, who was banished from

China. The ancient scripts talk about his deadly weapon, powerful enough to destroy the Great Wall of China and bring our country to its knees!"

"You think the football is a weapon?" said Frankie, raising an eyebrow.

"Perhaps," said Lin. "According to legend, the warrior was immortal. The only way to stop him was to take his weapon far away and bury it beneath the ground. They imprisoned him beneath the Great Wall in a chamber for all time. When the football was discovered, it must have awoken him."

"So if he has the football again . . ." said Louise.

"He will try to destroy the Great Wall of China!" finished Frankie. "How can we stop him? He has a dragon."

A terrible roar cut through the air. Suddenly the room fell dark as something blocked the light. Frankie saw a flash of red and jumped up from his chair. Everyone gathered at the window. Crowds of people on the ground below were shouting and pointing. In the sky above them, another huge dragon swooped through the air. Its scales were scarlet across its back and wings, but its underside was golden.

"Of course," said the curator. "According to Chinese beliefs, for every *yin* there is a *yang*. This must be a good dragon. I definitely believe you now!"

With a soft hiss, the beast turned its head to Frankie and his friends. Frankie recalled how the man had jumped on to the dragon's back.

"How far is the Great Wall of China from here?" he asked.

"About fifty miles," said Louise. "Are you thinking what I'm thinking? We should hitch a ride." She nodded towards the dragon.

"*I* think you're both mad," said Charlie.

Frankie shrugged. "It's the only way we can catch up." He opened the window.

"Hey, what are you doing?" It was the security guard, looking through a glass panel at the top of the locked door.

Frankie climbed on to the window ledge and Louise passed Max to him. "You know I hate heights," said Max.

The curator's eyes grew wide. "Did that dog just . . . ?"

"No, you're hearing things," said Max. Louise and Charlie joined

46

Frankie on the sill, their legs dangling over the edge. The dragon hovered ten metres below.

"Ready, team?" said Frankie. Then he jumped.

CHAPTER 4

Frankie fell on to the rough scales, and scrambled to hold on. Charlie clung to Louise behind him . . .

The dragon shrieked and with two powerful strokes of its gleaming wings the creature flew away from the museum. Frankie looked back and saw the curator waving. If he hadn't been busy hanging on for dear life, he would have waved back. The dragon soared up and away. Soon the people below were like ants. Then they burst into a cloud that hid everything, whipped by an icy wind. Frankie's knuckles began to turn blue with cold, and Max trembled, his ears flattened again his head. Charlie's teeth were chattering.

"I hope it knows where it's going!" shouted Louise, patting the dragon's scales.

They broke back through the cloud and saw the city far below. Soon, all they could see were rolling fields. The giant wings heaved up and down, driving them through the air.

Frankie caught sight of a dot in the sky ahead. He squinted.

"It's the other dragon," he said, pointing. "We're catching up!"

In a couple of minutes, they'd drawn alongside the dragon. The huge creature turned its head and

eyed them coldly, but the man on its back stared straight ahead, the football clasped in front of him.

"Why are you doing this?" cried Frankie over the rushing wind.

The man laughed deeply. "Zha-Hu will have revenge!" he boomed. The black dragon suddenly lashed its tail, catching the red dragon's wing. With a screech, the dragon veered away, almost tossing Frankie off its back. The evil dragon dipped towards the ground into a valley. Green hills sped beneath them, but Frankie's creature righted itself and swooped down, gliding along a ridge.

"Where did they go?" he asked, looking around. Their enemy had vanished.

Frankie tugged on the scales and the dragon rose a little.

Then he saw it — the Great Wall.

"Wow!" said Charlie and Louise at the same time.

For once, Max was lost for words.

The tall stone structure threaded across the landscape, rising and falling with the hills. Frankie couldn't even imagine how it had been built. There were large square towers every few hundred metres.

"There!" said Louise.

Frankie's glance followed her pointing finger and he saw Zha-Hu standing on a patch of bare ground beside the wall. His dragon had disappeared.

"Take us down!" yelled Frankie, hoping their ride would understand.

The red dragon drew back its wings and hovered over the clearing, as if afraid to go closer.

"I think it's scared of the ball," said Louise.

The ancient warrior threw back his head in a roar of triumph. He kicked the ball hard into the air. It was coming straight at them! As it smashed into the dragon's belly, the creature beneath them vanished into thin air. Suddenly, Frankie felt himself tumbling to the ground.

He landed with a grunt, and saw his friends hit the earth beside him.

"Is everyone okay?" he asked, getting to his feet.

His friends nodded, and Max shook the dirt from his fur. "I'm not okay," he grumbled.

Frankie turned to Zha-Hu. He had to try to distract him, and he could only think of one way. "How about a game?" he said. "The winner gets to keep the ball."

"A game?" said Zha-Hu, his eyes suddenly twinkling. Frankie sensed him smiling beneath his helmet. "Very well."

The warrior spread his fingers and pressed them against two of the ball's panels. The panels began to glow a dull shade of green.

"What's he doing?" asked Charlie. "I don't like—"

The ground rumbled and two cracks appeared in the dry earth. Frankie staggered back but managed to stay on his feet.

As the splits widened, shapes emerged from the ground, side by side. They seemed to be made from grinding plates of orange stone, covered in cracks. As they climbed out from beneath the ground, Frankie realised that one was a tiger and the other was a rat. Both were the size of his dad's car.

"They're creatures of the Chinese Zodiac," said Louise. "Made of terracotta clay!"

"The curator didn't mention that!" said Max.

Zha-Hu leapt on to the tiger's back in a single bound. "Enjoy your *game*," he said. "I have a wall to destroy." The tiger sprang away, claws digging into the earth, heading for the Great Wall.

The mammoth rat turned to face Frankie and his friends.

"I don't like rats even when they're smaller than me," muttered Louise.

The rat bared its teeth then bounded towards them, shaking the ground with every step. It was faster than a galloping horse.

As it headed towards them, Frankie and Louise dived one way, Charlie and Max the other. The rat screeched as it shot past, skidding into a tree. Frankie noticed a crack spreading over its flank.

"I think I know how we can

defeat it!" he said. "Quick, to the wall!"

He began to run, but straight away he heard the pounding steps of the terracotta rat behind him. He pumped his legs faster. Max scampered ahead. "Hurry up, Frankie!" he said.

Frankie didn't need to be told. He could see the beast's monstrous shadow closing over him. He'd almost reached the wall. *If this doesn't work, I'll end up squished!*

He smelled the rat's breath, dusty and sour, blasting over him. The wall was just ten metres away. Frankie put on a final burst of speed, and sprinted at it, letting his feet climb the wall. He managed six steps upwards, then pushed off in a backwards somersault. The rat didn't have time to stop. Frankie heard a crash as the rat smashed into the stone and exploded into fragments of terracotta. Max sniffed at one of the pieces.

Frankie's chest was rising and falling hard.

"No time to rest," said Louise. "Zha-Hu's already on the wall."

As soon as the words left her mouth, a low rumble sounded from all around and the ground trembled.

"Was that an earthquake?" asked Charlie.

Louise was pale. "I think that was Zha-Hu trying to destroy the wall!" she said.

Frankie looked up at the Great Wall of China. It had stood here for over two thousand years. If he didn't act quickly, this might be the day it came crashing down!

CHAPTER 5

They found a set of steps in the
outside of the wall, and dashed to
the top. Close up, it was more like
the battlements of a castle than a
simple wall, about twenty metres
across.

BOOM!

The structure shook, and spidery

cracks spread out beneath Frankie's feet.

"We don't have long," said Frankie. "Look, there he is!"

Zha-Hu was standing in the middle of the wall with his back to them and the ball on the ground in front of him. He lashed a fierce shot towards one of the towers.

Stone and dust exploded and

a large section of the tower crumbled. The cracks widened beneath Frankie as the ball rolled back to Zha-Hu.

"I don't understand," he said. "How can the football be so powerful?"

"It's magic, silly," said Max. "Just like yours!"

Zha-Hu turned to them and gave a mocking laugh. "Ancient magic," he said. "With the power to lay ruin not just to this wall, but to all of China."

He drew back his foot again, ready to direct another kick.

Max was a blur as he closed the distance between them and clamped his teeth across the warrior's ankle. Zha-Hu let out a yowl and flicked his leg, sending Max spinning high into the air. Frankie leapt forward and caught his little dog.

"You cannot stop me!" cried Zha-Hu, picking up the ball. As he pressed his fingers against the panels again, three more creatures materialised in front of Frankie and his friends, all made of overlapping plates of terracotta. There was a giant monkey, a snake almost forty feet long, and a lumbering ox, its stone flanks heaving.

"More creatures of the zodiac!" said Louise, backing up.

"They look tougher than the Year Ten defensive line," said Charlie.

The monkey howled and reached out with a clawed stone hand. Frankie backed away just in time, but heard his sweatshirt tear as a jagged nail snagged the material.

The snake slithered towards them, its body rattling on the ground.

The ox's huge nostrils blasted air.

Frankie retreated with Louise and Charlie at his side.

"We need to get hold of that ball," said Frankie. "It's the only way we can stop him destroying the wall."

The snake edged towards them, an orange tongue flickering in the air like a rattle.

"Easier said than done," muttered Max. "There's no way we can get past those creatures!"

Zha-Hu's ball struck the tower again – *BAM!* – and this time the whole wall seemed to lean to one side as Frankie and his friends stood on top. *He's got one powerful kick!* Frankie thought.

Even the terracotta creatures seemed worried as cracks split the wall at their feet. The ox bellowed and stamped, only making the damage worse. Frankie leapt out of the way as a huge split opened up in the wall beneath the snake. The snake's body balanced over the drop, stretched wide. It hissed in distress, baring its fangs. The monkey started to run towards it, then stumbled, toppling over the edge. They heard him smash to pieces below.

"One down," said Max.

The snake hissed again with anger. It was trapped — unable to go backwards or forwards.

The ox raked the ground with his foreleg, on the other side of the crevasse. Beyond it, Zha-Hu was lining up another kick. They had to get past the ox to stop him.

Maybe we can make it fall too,
thought Frankie. *Bulls like red,
don't they?*

Frankie pulled off his ripped
sweatshirt. He was wearing his
football kit underneath.

BAM! The wall shook and the
crack widened.

Frankie dangled the torn red
fabric like a bullfighter's cape.

"What are you doing?" asked
Charlie. "He's going to charge!"

"I know!" said Frankie. "That's
the point."

He waved his sweatshirt back and
forth. The ox's hooves thundered
across the top of the wall towards

the gap, then it leapt into the air. Its front hooves made it over the chasm, but its rear ones didn't. With a bellow of anger, the ox fell into the hole and its body shattered into fragments along with the monkey.

"Good work," said Louise. "Must be your lucky shirt!"

Frankie looked down. He was wearing his favourite player's shirt, emblazoned with a number 8.

"What do you mean?" he asked.

"Eight is a lucky number in China," said Louise. "Didn't you know?"

Frankie shook his head. "We'll need all the luck we can get. Follow me."

He kept a safe distance from the snake's head, then ran quickly, jumping on to its back. Balancing carefully, he tiptoed over the chasm, using the snake as a bridge. Beneath his feet, its body felt like wobbling stepping stones. As he reached the far side, its tail slipped a little. It was going to fall.

"Quick!" said Frankie to the others. "Before it's too late!"

Louise scurried over, with Charlie just behind her. As Charlie hopped to the other side, the snake's tail slipped, and the long coiling body dropped into the gap.

"What about me?" barked Max, still trapped on the other side.

"You'll have to jump!" called Frankie.

Max ran up to the gap, then backed away. "It's too far!"

Frankie shot a glance behind him. Zha-Hu was lining up another shot and the tower was crumbling at the top. *No time to waste . . .* He turned back to Max.

"You can do it, boy!" said Frankie.

Max shook himself and charged, hurling himself over the gap with his legs outstretched. He made it by a whisker, skidding to a halt in front of Frankie.

There was a tremendous crash that shook Frankie's whole body, and they were all thrown to the ground.

Looking up, Frankie saw the tower wobbling dangerously. Along the length of the wall, stones were falling. It wouldn't be long before the whole thing collapsed.

"What are you going to do now?" said Charlie, staring at Frankie. "It looks like our luck's run out!"

Luck? thought Frankie. Charlie had just given him an idea. He turned to his friend, and peeled off his number 8 shirt.

"I'm not going to do anything," he said. "You are!"

CHAPTER 6

Charlie frowned. "Huh? Me?"

"That's right," said Frankie. "I need you to make the most important save of your life." He pointed towards Zha-Hu.

Charlie went pale. "You mean . . . stop *that* ball?"

Frankie nodded.

"I don't even have my gloves!" said Charlie.

Frankie held out his football shirt. "Wear this. It will give you good luck."

Charlie looked torn. Frankie knew it had been a hard week for him, letting in goals on the school team. But there was no one else who could stop Zha-Hu's ball.

Charlie slowly took off his old shirt and handed it to Frankie, pulling the number 8 shirt over his head. "Are you sure about this?" he said.

"We all are," said Louise, patting him on the back.

"Go for it, Charlie," said Max, wagging his tail.

Charlie's fists clenched and he hurried towards the half-ruined tower. As he ran past Zha-Hu, the warrior laughed.

"What's this?" he said. "You're sending this little child to stop the mighty Zha-Hu?"

Charlie stood in front of the tower and spread his arms.

"I've saved a penalty in the regional final!" he said. "I can stop anything you've got!"

Zha-Hu chuckled. "Are you ready, child? You'll be buried under the ruins of the wall, just like I was!"

"He's always ready!" shouted
Frankie and Louise together.

Zha-Hu unleashed a shot so quick
that the ball was just a blur. Charlie
dived sideways and his body jerked
backwards. He slammed into the
tower, throwing up a cloud of dust.
Frankie could only see him dimly,
lying on the ground, curled up.

"Charlie?" called Frankie. He looked at Louise, who stared back with panic in her eyes.

Then Charlie stirred. He rolled on to his knees and slowly climbed to his feet. As the dust cleared, Frankie saw he was clutching the ball to his chest, grinning proudly.

"I did it!" he gasped.

Zha-Hu growled in fury. "Give me back my ball!" he said. "Give it to me!"

Charlie spun the ball on his fingertip, like he did in training, then tossed it over Zha-Hu's head to Frankie.

"No way," Frankie said, neatly catching it. "You'll have to come and get it."

Zha-Hu stamped his foot. "Oh, I will!" he said. "You've forgotten about my little friend."

His tiger leapt up on to the wall out of nowhere, standing between Frankie and the armoured warrior. It lowered its snout and roared, swiping with a paw.

Frankie ducked as stone claws whistled over his head. He and his friends backed away, but behind them was the gaping crack in the wall. They were trapped. Fall into the chasm, or face the terracotta

beast? Zha-Hu leapt on to the
tiger's back.

"So are you going to give me the
ball?" he said.

Frankie looked into the tiger's
jagged jaws. He had an idea, but it
was a long shot.

"Okay," he said. "We give up."

"I'm glad you've seen sense," said
Zha-Hu.

"No!" cried Louise. "You can't let
him. He'll destroy the Great Wall of
China!"

"There's no choice," said Frankie.
"Here, Zha-Hu!"

He dropped the ball, and swung
his foot, hitting it crisply on the half-

volley. He half expected the ball to shatter, but to his surprise, it didn't even hurt his foot and flew straight at the tiger's mouth, just as he'd planned. *Crash!* The ball smashed into the tiger's fangs and disappeared down its throat. The stone creature made a choking sound, then cracks appeared across its body.

"No! What have you done?" yelled Zha-Hu.

Flakes began to drop from the tiger, then larger sections of stone. The animal collapsed in on itself, burying the football. At the same time, Zha-Hu's armoured body seemed to crumble. He tumbled

with a cry into the fragments on the ground. As more and more pieces fell, they buried the whole of his body. His voice faded to nothing as the dust settled. Soon, he had disappeared.

Frankie peered into the mound of broken terracotta.

"Do you think he's gone?" said Charlie.

Max sniffed at the debris. "I can't even smell him any more."

"Zha-Hu is nothing without the ball's magic," said Frankie. "We've defeated him!"

Louise was gazing out over the landscape. "But what about all that?" she said, pointing to the wall. In many places it had collapsed completely.

Frankie's heart sank. They might have defeated Zha-Hu, but the Great Wall of China was a ruin. This didn't feel like a victory.

Max was still sniffing at the rubble. "What's that?" he said, poking his nose at something. Frankie saw it too – a golden glow from deep inside. He felt a spike of fear. Could Zha-Hu be coming back for another fight?

But it was a round shape that rose through the pile of rubble. *The football!*

It hovered in the air before them, so bright that Frankie had to squint. It sent out rays of light in all directions.

"Look!" said Louise. "The wall!"

As the ball's magical rays shone out, the wreckage slowly rose from the ground. Mounds of rubble were rebuilding themselves into solid stone. The tower rose in front of them once again, looking perfectly new.

"It's even better than before!" said Charlie.

The same was happening all along the wall, until the stone glowed for miles as it followed

the line of the hills. Frankie and
his friends had broken the dragon
curse!

Frankie felt a drop of water on
his skin, and looked upwards. The
sky above the wall was perfectly
clear — not a single cloud. "Weird,"
he said, as another drop splashed
on his arm. Then suddenly it was
pouring, the rain falling so thick and
fast he was soaked.

"We need to find shelter," he
said to the others. "Quick, to the
tower!"

They rushed across the top of
the wall, towards the rebuilt tower.
There was a door at the bottom,

and he pushed it open and bundled
through.

"Where are we?" gasped Charlie.

Frankie looked around him,
struggling to understand. There
were rows of students in kung
fu outfits like Louise's, all going
through a series of stretches. The
walls weren't stone, but covered
in posters and Chinese writing.
There was a huge paper model of a
dragon, hanging from the ceiling.

"We're back in the Chinese
Cultural Centre!"said Louise.

Frankie looked down and saw
that he was clutching his bag again,
just like when he'd first arrived

at the Cultural Centre earlier. He opened the bag and saw his own football, safely inside.

"Louise, it's not like you to be late!" said a voice. Frank looked back up. Sifu Tan stood at the front of the class. "But it's good to see you've brought some newcomers. Maybe you could introduce them to the class?"

Frankie frowned. Sifu Tan was acting like he'd never met them before. He looked back to the door, expecting to see the Great Wall of China, but it was just the street outside.

"Sorry," said Louise, bowing.

"We got a little bit delayed. This is Frankie and Charlie, and Max the dog."

The teacher didn't look impressed, especially when Max shook all the water from his fur. "Well, I hope you and your friends are ready to learn something about Chinese culture," said Sifu Tan.

Frankie grinned at his friends. "Oh, yes," he said. "We've learnt quite a bit already today!" They'd encountered a dragon, a Chinese warrior and Charlie had saved a goal from one of the first ever footballs.

"Come and join the class, then,"

said Sifu Tan. "We were just warming up."

Frankie took off his bag and placed it on the floor. This time the football was staying safely inside! He joined the other students with Charlie at his side.

"Ready to call yourself a goalie again?" he whispered to his friend.

Charlie smiled from ear to ear as he pulled his gloves back on. "Always!"

ACKNOWLEDGEMENTS

Many thanks to everyone at Little, Brown Book Group; Neil Blair, Zoe King, Daniel Teweles and all at The Blair Partnership; Luella Wright for bringing my characters to life; special thanks to Michael Ford for all his wisdom and patience; and to Steve Kutner for being a great friend and for all his help and guidance, not just with the book but with everything.

FRANKIE'S MAGIC FOOTBALL

Could you be a winner, like Frankie?

Take a look at the pictures in this book. Somewhere, we have hidden a miniature Chinese flag, just like this one:

Can you find it?

For the chance to win an exclusive Frankie's Magic Football goodie bag, write down the page number this secret image appears on then visit www.lbkids.co.uk/frankie chinacomp and ask a grown up to help you fill in the form.

Once you've completed your entry, you will be able to download a template to colour in your own Chinese flag.

This competition is open to all readers. Closing date is 30th October 2014. For full terms and conditions, see the website.

Frankie wishes you all good luck. Remember, everyone has talent!

FRANKIE'S MAGIC FOOTBALL

Have you read all of these adventures?

Tick the ones you have!

FRANKIE AND THE WORLD CUP CARNIVAL

Frankie and his team love playing football. There's always time for a game – especially when it's the World Cup!

But teams from round the world are playing disastrously so Frankie is transported to Brazil in order to save the tournament from ruin. He and his friends have to face up to jungle alligators, a Rio carnival and cheating opponents in order to help football superstar, Ricardo, rescue the trophy.

Can Frankie and his team save the World Cup in time for the final?

FRANKIE'S MAGIC FOOTBALL WEBSITE

Have you had a chance to check out **frankiesmagicfootball.com** yet?

Get involved in **competitions**, find out **news** and **updates** about the series, play **games** and watch **videos** featuring the author, **Frank Lampard!**

Visit the site to join **Frankie's FC** today!